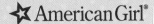
American Girl®

WellieWishers™

Ashlyn's Fall Fiesta

Adapted by Meredith Rusu
from the screenplay by Kati Rocky

Scholastic Inc.

ISBN 978-1-338-25429-7

10 9 8 7 6 5 4 3 2 1   18 19 20 21 22

Printed in the U.S.A. 40
First printing 2018

Book design by Carolyn Bull

Animation art direction by Jessica Rogers
and Riley Wilkinson

Scholastic Inc.
557 Broadway, New York, NY 10012

The wind is blowing.

The leaves are changing colors.

Fall has come to the garden.

And that means it's time for a party:

Ashlyn's Fall Fiesta!

Ashlyn makes sure everything is just right.

On the other side of the garden,
Ashlyn's friends read their invitations.
Ashlyn made them in the colors of
their coats.

Camille's invitation is blue.

Emerson's is purple.

Kendall's is pink.

And Willa's is red.

"Of course the invitations match our outfits," Camille says. "Ashlyn always thinks of everything."

"Come on!" Kendall says. "Let's go to the party!"

The WellieWishers arrive.
"Welcome to my Fall Fiesta!" Ashlyn says.
"Wow!" The WellieWishers gasp.

Everything looks amazing!
The napkins are perfectly folded.
The decorations are beautiful.
And the food smells delicious.
The WellieWishers take their
seats at the table.

Just then, a gust of wind blows by. The napkins start flying away.

"Oh, no!" cries Ashlyn. "We can't have a party without napkins!"

"Don't worry," Kendall says. "We'll get them back. Follow those napkins!"

The WellieWishers race after them.

Meanwhile, Ashlyn checks on her balloons. She is glad the wind hasn't messed them up.

Then she looks for spare napkins. "A good party planner is always prepared. I must have extra napkins here somewhere."

Over by the flower patch, the other WellieWishers chase after the napkins.

"First one to catch a napkin wins!" Willa cheers.

"Bingo-bango! I got mine!" Kendall laughs.

"Me, too!" says Camille.

"Look!" Emerson says. "The wind is making this napkin do a little dance."

She bows to the napkin like a ballerina. Then she leaps up and nabs it.

In no time, the WellieWishers have rounded up all the napkins.

Back at the party, Ashlyn is worried. "I couldn't find any extra napkins," she says.

"It's okay," Kendall says. "We caught them all. Chasing them was fun!"

"Whew!" Ashlyn says. "Now
the party can go on."
Everyone sits down again and
takes a yummy sandwich.

Suddenly, another gust of wind blows by.
This time, the balloons fly away.

"Not my decorations!" Ashlyn shouts.
"The wind is ruining everything!"

"Here we go again!" Kendall laughs.
"Follow those balloons!"

The girls whoop as they chase the
decorations. They catch all the balloons.
But on their way back to the party . . .
POP! POP! Some of the balloons burst.

Ashlyn is sad when her friends tell her about the balloons.

"My Fall Fiesta is turning into a Fiesta Fail," she groans.

"Cheer up," Kendall says. "We're having fun chasing things in the wind."

Ashlyn sighs. "I guess so. At least we still have the cake. Won't you please take your seats?"

But before they can sit down, a super-strong gust of wind blows by.

SMASH! A chair tips into the cake.

SQUASH! The cake falls over.

SPLAT! Cake frosting lands on Willa's face!

"That's it!" Ashlyn shouts. "The wind has ruined everything. My Fall Fiesta is officially over!"

"But we haven't had any cake yet,"
Willa says, as she licks some frosting
off her face. "It's delicious! You guys
have to try some!"

Emerson, Camille, and Kendall join her.
They grab some cake with their hands.

"Yum!" Camille says. "This is the best
cake ever!"

"You guys, the cake is supposed to be on
plates!" Ashlyn insists.

But her friends are having so much fun, they don't hear her.

"Willa, you have cake on your nose!" Camille giggles. "You look silly!"

"Oh yeah?" Willa smooshes some cake on Camille's face. "Now we're silly twins!"

"Come on," Emerson says to Ashlyn.
"Have some fun with us!" Then she
smooshes cake on Ashlyn's face!

The others gasp.

Will Ashlyn be upset?

Ashlyn tries the cake.

"Mmmmm," she says. "The cake IS pretty tasty!"

Just then, the wind blows the napkins away all over again.

"Follow those napkins!" Kendall says.

Ashlyn joins in this time. The WellieWishers laugh, jump, and chase the napkins flying in the breeze.

"Who knew things going so wrong could be so much fun?" Ashlyn tells her friends. Then she gets an idea.

"You are all invited to a new party," she
says. "It's called the Whoop-It-Up Wind
Party! And I have just the perfect game.
I'll be right back!"

A few minutes later, Ashlyn shows her friends a kite she made from a napkin.

"Amazing," her friends say.

The WellieWishers spend the rest of the afternoon flying the napkin kites.

Ashlyn's Fall Fiesta didn't go as planned, but her Whoop-It-Up Wind Party goes just right!

Turn the page

for a paper doll of
Ashlyn!

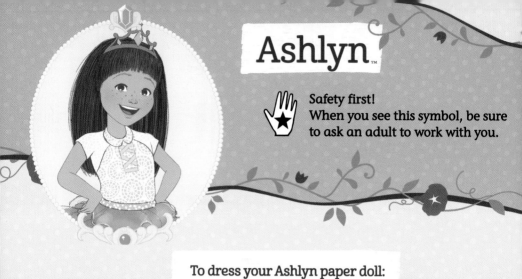

Ashlyn™

Safety first!
When you see this symbol, be sure to ask an adult to work with you.

To dress your Ashlyn paper doll:

1. Ask an adult to help you carefully cut out the clothing and accessories. Be sure to cut along all solid black lines, including slots.

2. Fold the tabs on the dotted lines and attach the clothing and accessories to your paper doll. Some tabs have slots to connect them together to help the clothes stay on better.

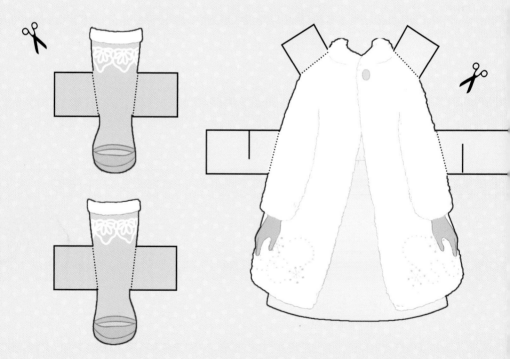

tabs on Ashlyn's play pieces can be folded back
ng the dotted lines to allow the items to stand up.

Want more
clothes for Ashlyn?

1. Use the cut-out clothes as stencils to
   trace blank clothes on paper.

2. Use colored pencils, markers, or
   even glitter and stickers to design
   your own outfits!

3. Ask an adult to help you cut out
   the clothes. Don't forget to leave
   tabs!

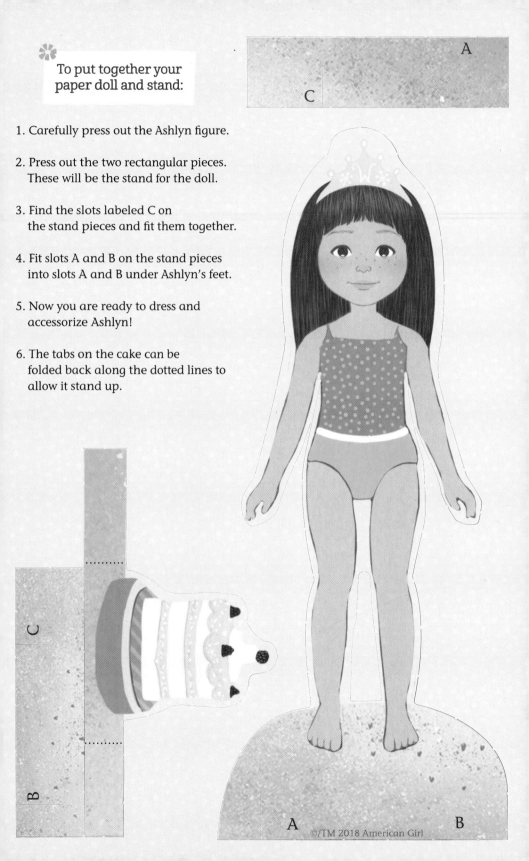

✳️ **To put together your paper doll and stand:**

1. Carefully press out the Ashlyn figure.

2. Press out the two rectangular pieces. These will be the stand for the doll.

3. Find the slots labeled C on the stand pieces and fit them together.

4. Fit slots A and B on the stand pieces into slots A and B under Ashlyn's feet.

5. Now you are ready to dress and accessorize Ashlyn!

6. The tabs on the cake can be folded back along the dotted lines to allow it stand up.

A

C

C

B

A

B